THE KING'S FOUNTAIN

LLOYD ALEXANDER

ILLUSTRATED BY
EZRA JACK KEATS

E. P. DUTTON   NEW YORK

A king once planned to build a magnificent fountain in his palace gardens, for the splendor of his kingdom and the glory of his name.

This fountain, however, would stop all water from flowing to the city below.

A poor man heard of it, and said to his wife:

"Soon our children will cry for water, our animals will sicken, and all of us will die of thirst."

His wife answered:

"A man of highest learning must go to the King, speak to him out of wisdom, and show him the folly of his plan."

So the poor man went throughout the city, to the most learned of scholars, and begged him to plead the cause.

But the scholar, deep in his own grand thoughts, barely listened. He pondered lofty matters and had no interest in humbler ones.

And the scholar lectured him with so many cloudy words that the poor man could make no sense of them at all, and went away downcast, saying to himself:

"Alas, the grandest thought quenches no thirst. Besides, what good is all the learning in the world if there is no one who can understand it?"

He realized that someone must present the cause clearly and winningly, with a golden tongue, so the King would listen and agree.

So he went to the marketplace, to the merchants whose words were smooth as pearls and who could string them together endlessly.

But when these merchants heard what he wanted, they choked with fear and their glib words failed them. While they gladly offered clever advice, not one dared face the King.

The poor man left them and went away dismayed, saying to himself:

"Alas, the finest words are empty air without the deeds to fill them. Besides, what good is a golden tongue without a brave heart"

Then he realized that a man of strength and courage must go and force the King to change his plan.

Again he went throughout the city, to the strongest of all brave men: a fearless metalsmith who could knot an iron bar as easily as a shoestring.

The metalsmith, eager to stand against the King, swore that once inside the palace he would smash every window, crack every wall, and break the King's throne into firewood.

The poor man sadly shook his head, knowing the palace guards would strike down the rash metalsmith before he did even one of those deeds. And the King in his wrath would be all the more determined to build his fountain. So, leaving the metalsmith still pounding his fists, he went away in despair, saying to himself:

"Alas, the strongest hand is useless without a wise head to guide it. Besides, what good is all the bravery in the world if it serves no purpose?"

He trudged home, hopeless and heavy-hearted, and told his neighbors and his family that he could find no one to stop the building of the fountain.

His daughter spoke then, and said:

"But, Father—why not go yourself?"

Confused, unable to answer, the poor man looked at the faces of his wife and family. At last, he bowed his head and murmured:

"I hear my own flesh and blood. Indeed, there is no one else, and I must must go to the King."

The poor man left his home. Alone, he slowly climbed the steep and seemingly endless hill.

Finally, he reached the King's high palace and for a long while stood outside, fearful and hesitant.

When the palace guards roughly seized him and threatened his life for intruding, the poor man trembled in such terror he could scarcely speak. Desperately he blurted out that he had an important message for the King alone.

The guards marched him to the throne room, where the King angrily demanded why he had come.

Knees knocking, teeth chattering, the poor man began to tell as well as he could of the suffering that the fountain would cause.

"Enough!" roared the King. "How dare you question what I do? I am the King!"

The poor man wished for the smallest crumb of the scholar's learning, but he could only stammer:

"Majesty—thirst is thirst, a poor man's no less than a king's."

Then his tongue dried in his mouth and he wished for even one of the merchants' golden words.

The King looked scornfully at him. "You come to trouble me for that? I need only snap my fingers and my swordsmen will cut you to pieces and be done with you."

The poor man wished for one drop of the metalsmith's bravery. With his own last ounce of courage, he answered:

"You have the power to kill me. But that changes nothing. Your people will still die of thirst. Remember them each time you see your splendid fountain."

The King started up, ready to call his guards. But he stopped and fell silent for a time, his frowns deep as his thoughts. Then he replied:

"You are too simple for clever debate with me; but you have a wiser head than a scholar. Your speech is halting; but there is more true eloquence in your words than in the golden tongue of a cunning counselor. You are too weak to crack a flea; but you have a braver heart than anyone in my kingdom. I will do as you ask."

The poor man returned to the city and told the news to all. The scholar wrote a long account of the matter in one of his books, and misplaced it. The merchants never stopped ornamenting tales of the poor man's deed. The metalsmith was so excited he tossed his anvil into the air and broke one of his own windows.

The poor man, glad simply to be home with his rejoicing family, was hardly able to believe what he had done.

"A wise head? A golden tongue? A brave heart?" he said to himself. "Well, no matter. At least none of us will go thirsty."

Unicorn is a registered trademark of E. P. Dutton.

Library of Congress number 72-133109   ISBN 0-525-44537-4

Originally published in the U.S. 1971 by
E. P. Dutton & Co.

First Unicorn Edition 1989 by
E. P. Dutton, a division of
Penguin Books USA Inc.

Published simultaneously in Canada by
Fitzhenry & Whiteside Limited, Toronto

Printed in Hong Kong by South China Printing Co.
10 9 8 7 6 5 4 3 2 1